DISNEP

WRECK-IT RALPH

I'm Gonna Wreck It!

randomhouse.com/kids

ISBN: 978-0-7364-2958-0 (trade)
ISBN: 978-0-7364-8117-5 (lib. bdg.)

Printed in the United States of America
10 9 8 7 6 5 4 3 2 1

I'm Gonna Wreck It!

Adapted by **Barbara Bazaldua**

Illustrated by **David Gilson**

Golden® First Chapters

𝕘 A GOLDEN BOOK • NEW YORK

My name is Wreck-It Ralph. Where I come from, there are only two kinds of guys: Good Guys and Bad Guys. What kind of guy am I? Well, I'm nine feet tall. I weigh 643 pounds. I'm always yelling, "I'M GONNA WRECK IT!" Kind of makes me a Bad Guy.

I live inside a video game called *Fix-It Felix Jr.,* along with a bunch of other characters called Nicelanders. Wrecking stuff is my job, and I'm good at it. In our game, Fix-It Felix fixes everything I break. He's the Good Guy.

So now that you know a little about me and where I come from, let me tell you about an adventure that changed my life. It's a pretty crazy story about some Good Guys, some Bad Guys, a cute kid, and lots of gooey taffy.

Not so long ago, I was going through a rough patch in life. Not only was I a Bad Guy, I was a sad Bad Guy. You see, the Nicelanders have always loved Felix. They made him pies. He got medals. Have I ever won a medal? Nope, not a single one. Instead, I got thrown off the roof and into the mud. It was dirty, boring, and lonely.

Don't get me wrong. I've always appreciated the fact that *Fix-It Felix Jr.* has been in Litwak's Family Fun Center for a long time. I've seen a lot of games in the arcade come and go. Sometimes they broke or got replaced with new ones. And once a game was unplugged, its characters became homeless.

So, yeah, I realized how lucky I was. I wasn't complaining. It just starts to feel hard

to love your job when no one else seems to like you for doing it. Well, maybe I am complaining—just a little.

One day, I decided it was time to attend a Bad-Anon meeting. The meetings gave Bad Guys from all the arcade games a place to feel good about being Bad.

"Just because you are a Bad Guy does not mean that you are a *bad guy*," of the members told me. "You can't change who you are."

"Maybe I don't want to be a Bad Guy anymore," I replied.

That really shocked them! They were worried I was "going Turbo," which is just about as bad as having your game shut down—maybe even worse.

At the end of the meeting, we stood in a circle and repeated the Bad Guy Affirmation: "I am Bad. And that's good. I will never be Good. And that's not bad. There's no one I'd rather be than me."

But it didn't make me feel any better. No one understood. I just wanted to be appreciated, have some nice friends, and get a medal—was that too much to ask?

CHAPTER
02

After the meeting, I traveled along the power cords to Game Central Station, where all the games in the arcade are connected. The minute I stepped off the train, Surge Protector stopped me and asked for identification. He does it every time.

"You know my name," I told him. I was in no mood to cooperate.

"Anything to declare?" he asked.

"I hate you," I answered.

That seemed to prove that I was who I said I was, so he let me pass.

Game Central was busy, as usual, with characters coming and going, chatting about how their day had gone. No one

asked me if I'd had a nice day. Typical.

I stopped to give a couple of homeless characters some snacks. These poor guys didn't have a home because their games were out of order. Whenever that happens, video game characters are forced to flee to Game Central. It's a real bummer.

I headed into the tunnel that led to *Fix-It Felix Jr.* and my home not-so-sweet home.

I live in a pile of bricks in the town dump. I've furnished it tastefully with a stump. It's not much, but it's mine. Felix lives in a fancy penthouse apartment.

That night, I sat on my stump and watched everyone enjoying the thirtieth anniversary party for our game.

"Happy anniversary for everyone but Ralph," I muttered. Then I saw some characters from other video games at the party.

Felix had invited those guys? They weren't even part of our game! That was just too much to bear . . . even for a big guy like me.

"I am going!" I said. **"I AM GOING TO THE PARTY!"**

I walked right up to the penthouse and knocked on the door. Felix seemed surprised to see me. I told him I had heard an explosion and had come to see if everything was all right.

"Oh, those were fireworks," Felix explained. "We're—uh—throwing a party for the game's thirtieth anniversary."

"Oh, is that tonight?" I asked innocently.

Just then, someone shouted that the cake was ready.

"Cake!" I said. "I love cake."

"I don't suppose you'd want to have a slice," Felix offered.

I supposed I did. So Felix invited me inside.

No one welcomed me, but I kept smiling. I thought if I acted friendly, they might realize I wasn't such a bad guy—for a Bad Guy.

Then I saw the cake. It was shaped like the building in our game. All the party guests oohed and aahed. A little figure of Felix stood on the roof, surrounded by figures of the other Nicelanders. Felix was reaching for a medal. My little figure was sitting in the mud.

"This little guy would be a lot happier if you put him up here with everyone else," I said. I put my Ralph figure on top of the cake. I moved the Felix figure into the mud. Then I put the medal on the Ralph figure.

"But Bad Guys don't win medals," said Roy, one of the Nicelanders.

"Well, suppose I could win a medal. Then you'd let me up here, right?" I asked.

"If you win a medal, we'll let you *live* up here," said Gene, another Nicelander. "But it will never happen, because you're just the Bad Guy who wrecks the building."

I felt my temper rising.

"No, I'm not!" I answered. I slammed my fist down on the cake. Chunks flew everywhere.

"Yes, you are," said Gene.

All the Nicelanders glared at me. I wanted to say something, but I had a feeling I had done enough. I hung my head and walked out the door.

CHAPTER 03

Along with the cake, I had just smashed any chance of being invited to a party for the rest of my life. I was feeling as down as a wrecked building. So I visited a restaurant in another video game and ordered a mug of root beer. I sat alone, feeling glum. Where was I going to get a medal?

I thought the server might know, so I asked him. He suggested looking through the Lost and Found. As I was digging through the box, a soldier walked by—and kept on walking—straight into the wall.

His name was Markowski, and he was from a new game called *Hero's Duty*. He was also a shaking, trembling, nervous wreck.

"We've only been plugged in a week. Every day, it's climb the tower. Fight bugs. Climb the tower. Fight more bugs," said Markowski.

"It's tough all over," I said.

Markowski just ignored me and continued. "And for what? A lousy Medal of Heroes," he muttered with glazed eyes.

That got my attention.

"Is there any chance I could go with you to your game?" I asked.

"Negatory," Markowski replied. "*Hero's Duty* is only for the best and the brave— *AAAHH!*" He saw a cockroach scuttle across the table. He screamed and passed out.

I quickly "borrowed" his uniform and helmet and headed over to *Hero's Duty.* I thought I could go into the game, win a medal, and be back before anyone missed me. How hard could it be?

The answer is . . . hard. Oh, I made it into the game easily enough. No one realized I wasn't Markowski. A player put a coin into the game, and the timer began counting down to the moment when the game started. I was sitting with a bunch of other soldiers in the dark, just waiting. I was feeling pretty sure of myself as I watched a monitor on a rinky-dink robot with wheels. It showed an image of a little girl—the first-person shooter. The platoon leader, a tough-as-nails woman named Sergeant Calhoun, stepped in front of her.

"We are humanity's last hope," Calhoun said to the first-person shooter. "Our mission: destroy all cy-bugs. Are you ready, rookie?"

The door opened, and I gasped. This was nothing like my game. A forbidding tower rose over a dark, twisted landscape teeming with giant bugs.

What had I done?

"Cy-bug, twelve o'clock!" Calhoun shouted as a giant bug bore down on me, pincers snapping. I shot at it—and missed. I had terrible aim, and this had been a horrible idea!

I ran left. I ran right. There were bugs everywhere. I aimed at one, but it ate my blaster! I watched, horrified, as its pincers transformed into blasters themselves. Then it started firing at me. Sweet Mother Hubbard! These creatures morphed into whatever they ate! Calhoun destroyed a bug just before it could turn me into its midday snack.

"Get back in formation," Calhoun ordered. "The entrance to the lab is right across that bridge." She pointed to the tower.

It looked like a safe place to hide. I dashed toward it. Big mistake. As I ran, I set off motion sensors, and the lab doors flew open. Swarms of cy-bugs poured out. There was no place to run . . . no place to hide. Oh, wait—yes, there was!

I ducked behind the first-person shooter.

"Save me! Save me!" I screamed as a cy-bug attacked the little girl.

"Game over!" said the game narrator. But the cy-bugs kept attacking. They didn't stop fighting when the game was over, like Bad Guys are supposed to. It was like the cy-bugs didn't know—or didn't care—that they were part of a game.

A beacon of light flashed from the tower. Instantly, the cy-bugs stopped attacking and turned to the light as if they had been hypnotized. Thousands of them rose into

the air and zoomed toward the beacon.
ZAP! Bye-bye, bugs.

Calhoun stormed over.

"**NEVER** interfere with the first-person
shooter!" she shouted.

She ordered me back to the start position,
but I had a better idea. The medal was at
the top of the tower. To get it, I could either
fight through all that bug-infested chaos, or
I could climb for it. I didn't care if I was

following actual game-play rules. Litwak's Family Fun Center was just about to close. By the time it opened the next morning, I would be a Good Guy with a shiny medal!

CHAPTER 04

Meanwhile, in the *Fix-It Felix Jr.* game, the Nicelanders were panicking because I wasn't there to wreck the building for Felix to fix. A kid playing the game told Mr. Litwak, the arcade owner, that the game was busted, and Mr. Litwak slapped an OUT OF ORDER sign on the screen.

If the game was out of order, there was a chance it would be unplugged and carted away. If the Nicelanders were in the game when that happened, they would be doomed. So they only had two choices: find me before the arcade opened, or flee to Game Central.

"Fix it, Felix!" the Nicelanders begged.

Felix had a difficult time calming everyone down. He assured them that he'd find me and bring me back. Another video game character gave Felix a tip. He told him I had gone to *Hero's Duty*.

When Felix arrived in *Hero's Duty*, Sergeant Calhoun nearly attacked him.

"Who the holy hotcakes are you?" she asked.

"I'm Fix-It Felix Jr., ma'am. Have you by any chance seen my friend Ralph?"

Then Felix glanced at the tower. He called my name, but I didn't hear him. I could see the gleaming medal floating in the center of the room. I could almost feel it in my hands. I climbed through a window and landed on the laboratory floor. It was covered in cy-bug eggs—thousands of them. *Eyuk.*

One false step and *CRUNCH.*

I took a deep breath and started tiptoeing. "You can do it. Don't blow it," I muttered.

The medal floated before me. My fingers closed around it. It was mine! I put it around my neck.

"Congratulations, soldier!" the game announcer exclaimed.

I had done it! My future lit up like a game screen. I envisioned friends . . . parties . . . cakes with cute little figures of ME on top!

CRUNCH!

Whoops. I stepped on an egg and it broke open. Then I froze as a baby cy-bug scurried out. It flew at me and sank its pincers into my face!

"Ah! Get off!" I yelled.

I stumbled backward into an open space pod. The doors shut, and the pod roared to life. It zoomed out of *Hero's Duty* and rocketed down the tunnel into Game Central. Sergeant Calhoun and Felix ran after me, but I didn't see them. I was too busy trying to pry the cy-bug off my face.

The pod ricocheted around Game

Central and entered a dark tunnel. Gobs of pink goo splattered the windshield.

Seconds later, the pod crashed to a stop. My face hit the eject button and I catapulted out into a tree. Luckily, the impact finally ripped the cy-bug loose.

"*Sayonara,* sucker," I muttered as I watched it hit the ground and sink into a deep pool of—TAFFY?

Mother Hubbard! Where was I?

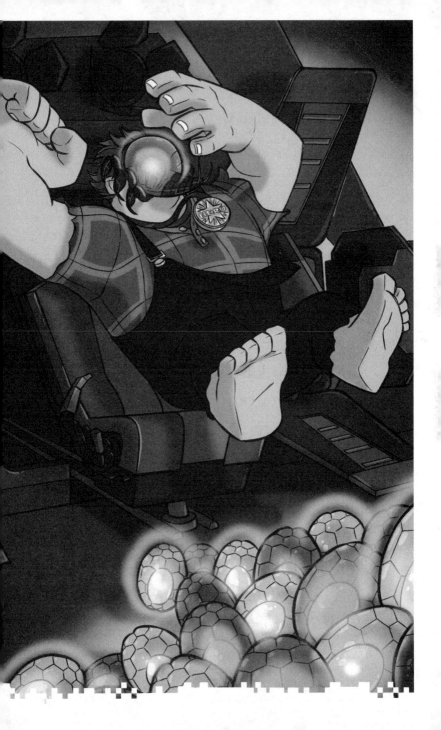

A sugar-coated landscape with frosted mountains, lollipop trees, and cotton candy clouds surrounded me.

Oh, man! I had crash-landed in that silly candy kart racing game, *Sugar Rush*. I had to get out of there and back to the arcade before it opened. But with the pod destroyed, I had a long walk home.

At that moment, I saw something glimmering at the top of a tree.

My medal! It must have come off when I landed. I had to get it back.

Okay, Ralph, I told myself. *Stay calm. Just climb the tree, get the medal, and hoof it back home.*

I'd made it halfway up, when—

"Hello!"

A squeaky voice greeted me from a high branch.

I looked up. The voice belonged to a little girl. She was peering down, grinning.

"Are you a hobo?" she asked.

"No, I am not a hobo," I told her. "But I am busy, so go home."

"Whatcha doing here?"

She sure was a nosy kid.

"I'm from the candy tree department. Just doing some routine candy-cane tree trimming," I told her. I was trying to be nice, but then she started mimicking everything I was saying.

Great. She wasn't just a nosy brat; she was a rude brat, too. I kept climbing.

Just then, the brat saw the medal.

"A gold coin!" she exclaimed.

"That's mine!" I yelled as she scampered up the branches.

I grabbed a double-stripe peppermint branch. It broke and I fell, but I caught myself and scrambled back up toward the brat—just as she snagged my medal.

I lunged for the medal. The brat dropped it. I caught it. She dove for it. I landed on another double-stripe branch. *CRACK!* Down I went again. The medal flew from my hands. The brat snagged it. Suddenly, she started to flicker. For a second, she seemed to disappear. Then she reappeared on a branch below me. She was glitching!

"Give me back my medal!" I pleaded as she swung down from the tree. "Look, that thing is my ticket to a better life." I tried to appeal to her kinder instincts. Too bad she didn't have any.

"Well, now it's *my* ticket," she said. "So long, chump!" As she ran off, the double-stripe branch I was dangling from broke, and I landed—*PLOP!*—in the taffy swamp.

"I will find you!" I shouted as the brat disappeared over the hill toward the racetrack. But I wasn't sure she heard me. My mouth was too full of goo to speak clearly.

While I struggled out of the taffy pool, the brat reached the racetrack. King Candy, the ruler of Sugar Rush, was announcing the rules of the Random Roster Race. The racers had to toss a coin into a gold cup to have their names entered. The first nine contestants to cross the finish line would be on the racer list in the actual arcade game. The racers competed every night to qualify, but this was the first time the little brat had a coin. If she was one of the racers who crossed the finish line, she would be allowed to race in the game.

King Candy tossed his coin first. It clanged into the cup and his name appeared in lights on the board. One by one, the other racers threw their gold coins in, and their names appeared: Taffyta Muttonfudge, Minty Zaki, Adorabeezle Winterpop, Snowanna Rainbeaux, Jubileena Bing-Bing, Gloyd Orangeboar, Crumbelina Di Carmello, Rancis Fluggerbutter, Swizzle Malarkey, and Candlehead.

At last, it was the brat's turn. She threw MY medal into the cup. *CLANG!* Her name appeared on the board: Vanellope von Schweetz. She was in the race!

There was just one problem. Vanellope

was missing some of her code, which made her flicker. She was considered a glitch—and King Candy had declared that glitches could never, ever race.

"Security! Security!" King Candy shouted. Two Donut Police officers ran toward Vanellope. They were about to grab her when I barreled onto the track, dripping taffy.

"GIMME BACK MY MEDAL!" I bellowed. Vanellope ducked under the stands and I followed, which made them come crashing down. Vanellope got away, but a giant cupcake fell on me.

King Candy announced that the race would be held later, after they cleaned up the mess I had made. Then he and his Donut Police dragged . . . er . . . rolled me away.

CHAPTER 06

The Donut Police rolled me into King Candy's castle. Sour Bill, King Candy's assistant, peeled the taffy off my face so he could see who I was. It hurt.

"Wreck-It Ralph? What are you doing in my game?" King Candy exclaimed. "You're not going Turbo on us, are you?

"You people have my medal!" I snarled. "I want it back!"

"It's not yours anymore," King Candy explained. "The glitch—Vanellope—threw it in the cup, and the coins in the cup go to the winner of the race."

"I'm not leaving without my medal!" I exclaimed.

But King Candy didn't care about me or my medal. He wanted to stop Vanellope.

"Get our guest cleaned up and out of my game," he ordered the Donut Police. "I have a glitch to deal with."

Then he drove away.

But I wasn't giving up. I broke out of the cupcake, crashed through a wall, and took off.

It didn't take me long to track down that medal-snitching brat. I found the little crumb-snatcher working on her ridiculous handmade kart.

But before I could reach her . . . *Vroooom!*

Some racers roared around the bend and skidded to a stop. The leader, Taffyta, strolled over to Vanellope.

"You have to back out of the race," Taffyta said. "Glitches may never, ever, ever, ever race."

"I'm not a glitch, Taffyta," Vanellope protested. "And I'm definitely racing!"

At Taffyta's signal, the other racers threw Vanellope in the mud. Then they started smashing her kart.

I wasn't crazy about the kid taking my medal, but seeing everyone gang up on her like that made me angry. It was just uncool. Uncool.

"Get out of here, you little cavities!" I shouted, running down the hill and waving my arms at the bullies. They scattered, screaming.

Vanellope was picking up the pieces of her broken kart and trying not to cry.

"What are YOU looking at?" she asked, sniffling.

"You're welcome, you rotten little thief," I answered.

"I'm not a thief. I just borrowed your stupid coin. I was gonna give it back to you as soon as I won the race."

But even I knew there was no way Vanellope was going to win the race in her rickety little kart.

"I earned that medal, and you better get it back for me!" I said.

I was so angry, I punched a few jawbreaker boulders. It didn't help. But it seemed to give the little crumb-snatcher an idea.

"So here's what I'm thinking . . . ," she said. "You help me get a real kart, and I'll win the race and get you back your medal."

I guess she figured I was her only chance to win the race. And she was my only chance of getting my medal back. So I agreed.

"You had better win!" I told her, and shook her hand. I couldn't believe it. We were a team.

CHAPTER
07

I learned later that Felix and Sergeant Calhoun had followed my trail of destruction into *Sugar Rush*. They had found the escape pod. Immediately, Calhoun started scanning the area for cy-bugs.

"Cy-bugs are a virus," she told Felix. "Without a beacon to stop them, they'll consume *Sugar Rush*. Then they'll invade every other game until the arcade is nothing but a smoking husk of forgotten dreams."

Calhoun's cy-bug sensor started to beep. It directed them toward the taffy lake, where the cy-bug had landed.

"So, what's going on with Wreck-It?" asked Calhoun.

"He was acting kind of squirrelly," Felix replied. "But I never thought he'd do something like this. He knows what happened with Turbo."

Calhoun had never heard of Turbo, so Felix filled her in. *Turbo Time* had once been the most popular racing game in the arcade. The main character, Turbo, loved the attention—a little too much.

When a new racing game came along and stole Turbo's thunder, he was so jealous, he left his game and tried to take over the new one. But he ended up putting both games, and himself, out of order—for good.

"I can't let that happen to my game," said Felix.

"Don't worry," Calhoun said. "We'll find Wreck-It and get you home."

As Calhoun and Felix continued toward the taffy lake, they suddenly fell into a pit of cocoa powder! They began to sink fast. Taffy vines hung above them, but they were too high to reach.

Felix looked at a cocoa quicksand warning sign posted beside the pit. Even though his life was in danger, sinking into chocolate powder seemed very funny to Felix. He started to giggle. As his giggling turned to laughter, the vines above them began to lower. Felix thought for a moment. "You have to laugh to make the vines grow!"

"I don't laugh," said Calhoun.

"Here comes the tickle monster!" said

Felix. He reached over to Calhoun and tickled her.

Soon both of them were laughing uncontrollably. The vines grew until Felix and Calhoun could grab them. Then the vines retracted, lifting them out of the quicksand.

Felix and Calhoun gazed into one another's eyes. Just looking at Calhoun gave Felix a warm honey-glow feeling.

"That was quick thinking, Fix-It," said Calhoun, blushing a little. Then she checked her cy-bug sensor. "We lost the cy-bug," she continued. "C'mon, we've got to fix that shuttle."

Felix followed Calhoun, beaming from ear to ear.

CHAPTER 08

Meanwhile, Vanellope and I broke into the kart bakery. A screen lit up with all different kinds of karts.

"We gotta make one," said Vanellope.

"Bad idea, kid. I don't make things, I break things," I said.

"Looks like you'll be stepping outside your comfort zone, then," said Vanellope as she selected a kart from the screen.

The bakery was actually a mini game that had three levels: selecting ingredients, baking, and decorating. Let's just say I messed up all three. When our finished kart rolled out on the conveyor belt, it was a mess.

"Kid, I tried to warn you . . . I don't make things, I—"

Vanellope cut me off. "I love it!" she shouted. Then she handed me a pastry bag. "A work of art like this must be signed!"

I had never made anything before. And I have to admit that as I wrote MADE BY RALPH on the back of the kart, I felt proud.

Unfortunately, I didn't have much time to enjoy the feeling. Just then, King Candy and the Donut Police pulled up.

"It's the glitch and Wreck-It Ralph. Get them!" King Candy yelled.

It was time to go.

I threw Vanellope into the driver's seat of the kart and hopped on.

"I don't know how to drive a real kart," Vanellope admitted.

It wasn't the best time to hear that news. I pushed off with my hands and we sped away. King Candy and the Donut Police

were coming up fast behind us.

"Head for Diet Cola Mountain," Vanellope said, pointing to a sign. "Now drive into the wall!"

"What?" I yelled. "Are you crazy?"

"Just do it!" Vanellope commanded.

I aimed the kart at the mountain and waited for the crash. But it didn't come. Instead, we hit the wall, slid through a secret door, and disappeared from King Candy's sight.

We came to a stop in a damp, dim cavern full of half-built game props. A giant stalactite made of Mentos hung over a bubbling pool. When a piece of it broke and dropped into the Diet Cola Hot Springs, a steaming geyser shot up.

"Welcome to my home!" Vanellope announced. She showed me her bed made of old candy wrappers. "I bundle myself up like a little homeless lady," she said.

It was all too sad and familiar. I should

have felt sorry for her, but I was too angry.
The little glitch didn't even know how to
drive!

Vanellope insisted she was a racer. "I can
feel it in my code," she said.

I thought she was nuts. How in the
world was she going to *win* a race when she
didn't even know *how* to race?

CHAPTER 09

"That's it. I'm never getting my medal back," I said.

"What's the big whoop about that crummy medal anyway?" Vanellope asked.

I tried to explain. "In my game, I am the Bad Guy. I live in garbage and everyone hates me. That crummy medal was going to change all that."

"That's exactly what racing would do for me," Vanellope replied. "Everyone here says I'm a mistake and I shouldn't even exist."

"Why don't you leave?" I asked.

"Glitches can't leave their games," she answered bitterly. "It's one of the joys of being me."

Suddenly, I understood. She was an outcast like me. I guess that was when I stopped being angry and began to take her side.

I started to pound the rocks around us to make a racetrack.

"If you're gonna race, you need to learn how to drive," I told her.

"Awesome!" Vanellope shouted.

It was a little rough at first. Vanellope's enthusiasm and her skills didn't quite match. She stalled. She swerved. She drove into rocks. She tried a jump, but glitched and hit the stalactite. Bits of Mentos fell into Diet Cola Hot Springs, causing giant geysers to shoot up.

"Are you crazy?" I screamed. "You almost blew up the whole mountain! If you want to win, you have to get your glitching under control!"

Vanellope concentrated hard. She raced around curves and flew up ramps. I had to admit it—the girl was a natural.

For the first time, I thought maybe—just maybe—she had a chance at winning! But she had to learn how to control those glitches.

As we started to the racetrack, Vanellope turned and dashed back into the cavern.

"Forgot something!" she yelled.

As I watched her go, I felt proud—of both her and myself. It felt great to be able to help someone.

Just then, King Candy drove up. He held out my medal. I was shocked.

"It's yours. Go ahead, take it," he said.

I slowly took the medal from him.

"All I ask is that you hear me out," King Candy said.

"About what?" I asked.

"I need your help. Sad as it is, Vanellope cannot be allowed to race."

"Why are you people so against her?" I asked.

"I'm not against her. I'm trying to protect her," replied King Candy.

He went on to explain that if Vanellope crossed the finish line in the qualifying race, she would be added to the roster for the actual game, and kids could choose to race her. But when they saw her glitching, they would think the game was broken. *Sugar Rush* would be put out of order. Everyone but Vanellope could flee to Game Central.

"When the game's plug is pulled, she'll go down with it," King Candy finished.

He was right. I couldn't let Vanellope risk her life. I agreed to talk her out of racing.

"Very good," said King Candy. "Now I'll give you two some time alone."

After he drove off, Vanellope returned. I could barely look at her. Then, to make me feel much, much worse, she gave me a handmade heart medal. On the back she had written YOU'RE MY HERO.

I didn't feel like a hero. I felt like a jerk.

"You can't be a racer," I blurted out. But before I could finish, Vanellope saw the medal poking out of my pocket and yanked it away.

"You sold me out?" she cried.

I tried to explain how dangerous it was for her to race. But she wasn't listening. In her eyes, I was a traitor. She threw the medal in my face.

"I don't need you! I can win the race on my own!" She climbed into her kart.

I pulled her out. "I'm doing this for your own good," I said. Then I brought my fists down on the kart again and again.

"You really *are* a Bad Guy," she sobbed.

I watched Vanellope dash into the mountain. I picked up the medal and started home. Alone.

CHAPTER 10

It was quiet in the *Fix-It Felix Jr.* game. Too quiet. The Nicelanders weren't around to ignore me or snub me. Their apartments were dark except for a light shining in Felix's penthouse. The door was open, so I went in.

"Well, you actually did it," a voice said from the shadows. It was Gene, the Nicelander who had told me to get my own medal on the night of the thirtieth-anniversary party. "You won a medal."

"Where is everybody?" I asked.

"They're gone," he answered.

That was when I learned that Felix had gone to find me. When he hadn't come back, the Nicelanders had panicked and left the game. Now it was officially out of order. When the arcade opened in the morning, Mr. Litwak would pull the plug.

"This is not what I wanted," I told Gene.

"What did you want, Ralph?" he asked.

"I just . . . I was tired of living alone in the garbage."

Gene shrugged. "Well, now you can live alone in the penthouse," he replied.

After he left, I stared at my Medal of Heroes. It wasn't worth the harm I had caused trying to get it. I threw it at the game screen and knocked the OUT OF ORDER sign to one side. Now I could see the *Sugar Rush* game across the arcade.

I stared at it. Something didn't make sense. Vanellope's picture was on the game console. If she had always been a glitch . . . if she had never been meant to race . . . why was she there?

I was going to find out. I rushed back to *Sugar Rush* and found Sour Bill sweeping

up the pieces of Vanellope's kart. He refused to talk—until I threatened to lick him.

It took only a couple of licks before the cowardly cough drop agreed to tell me everything. As it turned out, Vanellope belonged in the game. King Candy had tried to delete her. But because he couldn't remove all of her code, she had become a glitch.

"He'll do anything to keep her from crossing that finish line, because if she does, the game will reset and she'll be a real racer," Sour Bill confessed. But he swore he didn't know why King Candy didn't want Vanellope to be a racer.

I had to find Vanellope and try to fix things. But Sour Bill told me it was too late. She was in the castle dungeon, along with Felix!

I hadn't even known Felix was in *Sugar Rush*. Later, I found out that he and Calhoun had split up. While Felix was searching for me, he happened upon King Candy's castle. Sour Bill saw Felix and sent him straight to the dungeon.

I raced to the castle and broke through the dungeon walls. At first, Felix wasn't happy to see me.

"Do you have any idea what you've put me through?" he scolded. "I ran all over creation looking for you. I met the most dynamite gal who rebuffed my affections, and then I got thrown in jail! You don't know what it's like to be rejected and treated like a criminal!"

"Yes, I do. That's every day of my life," I answered. "That's why I ran off and tried to be a Good Guy. But I'm not. And I need your help. There's a little girl whose only hope is this kart. Please, Felix, fix it!"

Felix smiled. Then he began to fix Vanellope's kart. He really was a good Good Guy.

When I broke down the door to Vanellope's cell, I didn't even give her a chance to yell at me.

"I know, I know, I know. I'm an idiot," I said.

"And?" said Vanellope.

"And a numbskull," I replied.

"And?"

"And a selfish diaper baby."

"And?"

"And a stink brain."

"The stinkiest brain ever," said Vanellope with a smile.

I quickly broke the chains and freed Vanellope. Then we hopped into the kart and took off for the racetrack.

I was feeling great! I really thought we had this race in the bag.

But little did I know, we had other problems. Sergeant Calhoun had been searching for cy-bugs and had stumbled upon a cavern full of them. And they were hungry!

The stands were jammed with cheering fans. Soda bottles sprayed fountains of foam. Popcorn boxes popped their tops.

King Candy stood in his royal box. "Let the Random Roster Race commence!" he announced. Then he jumped into his kart. The race was on!

As Vanellope, Felix, and I reached the track, I told Vanellope that she just needed to cross the finish line to be a real racer.

"I'm already a real racer," said Vanellope. Then she looked right at me. "And I'm going to win."

She zoomed off to catch up with the other racers. Taffyta and Candlehead tried

to stop her, but she glitched past them, causing them to crash into a stand of giant red velvet cupcakes.

Felix and I cheered for Vanellope at the finish line. Suddenly, Sergeant Calhoun showed up. Then hundreds of cy-bugs burst out of the ground!

All the *Sugar Rush* residents fled in horror as Calhoun ran off to fight the bugs. I stayed back to guard the finish line. I pummeled the cy-bugs with my fists, but they just kept coming.

Vanellope and King Candy were now in Nougat Mine. King Candy rammed into the front of Vanellope's kart.

"Get off this track!" he yelled.

As Vanellope tried to push King Candy away, she began to glitch. Her glitches made King Candy glitch, too. His whole appearance began to change. He was transforming into . . .

TURBO!

"Now look what you've done!" Turbo screamed. He floored the gas and pushed Vanellope's kart toward a center divider. She was seconds away from crashing!

Vanellope closed her eyes. "C'mon, glitch," she whispered to herself.

Then she did it! She disappeared and then reappeared in the right lane.

Turbo was shocked. He crashed into the center divider. Vanellope had the lead now, and it was a straight shot to the finish line.

"Bring it home, kid!" I yelled.

Then . . . *BOOM!*

A cy-bug burst from the ground, right in front of Vanellope's kart. She swerved, spun out, and crashed into the side of the track. Felix and I ran to her.

"Kid, are you okay?" I asked.

"I'm fine," Vanellope replied.

I turned back to look at the finish line. The cy-bugs had destroyed it.

As we ran toward the exit to Game

Central, Turbo emerged from the tunnel and saw the cy-bugs devouring everything in sight. "I'll get you, Ralph, if it's the last thing—"

A cy-bug crept up behind Turbo and opened its jaws. The cy-bug gobbled him up faster than you can say Turbo-tastic.

We were still in trouble. The cy-bugs
just kept coming. Felix and Calhoun were
already at the exit when Vanellope and I got
there. I tried to push her through the exit,
but she kept hitting an invisible wall.

"I told you, I can't leave the game," she
said. "Just go without me."

"No," I told her. "I'm not leaving you
here alone."

"There's nothing we can do without a
beacon," said Calhoun. "There's no way to
stop these monsters."

Then I remembered the beacon in *Hero's
Duty*. Attracting the cy-bugs to a strong
light and zapping them was the only way

to beat them. Suddenly, I had the most brilliant idea of my life.

"As soon as the bugs are dead, fix that finish line and get Vanellope across it," I told Felix. I jumped on a cruiser and flew toward Diet Cola Mountain. I was going to wreck it.

I landed on the crater on top of the mountain and started punching it. I could hear rumbles beneath my feet as pieces of the stalactite fell into Diet Cola Hot Springs

below. As I continued to pound with my fists, something grabbed me and lifted me into the air. It was a giant Turbo cy-bug. The bug that had eaten Turbo had turned into him! And now he was holding me in his pincers high above the mountain.

"Game over, Bad Guy," said Turbo as he tried to crush me.

With all my strength, I wrenched myself free and fell toward the crater.

"I am Bad. And that's good. I will never be Good. And that's not Bad. There's no one I'd rather be than me," I said. I held tightly to the medal that Vanellope had made for me. In a minute, it would all be over, but it was okay. I would have saved the game and Vanellope's life.

I hit the crater's center and crashed through it. The entire stalactite broke free and fell toward the pool, and I fell with it. Then something shot under me. I opened my eyes and saw Vanellope grinning. She

had glitched into the mountain in her kart and picked me up.

"Don't worry, I got it under control!" she shouted as we glitched out of harm's way and into a chocolate river far away from the mountain. Seconds later—*BOOM!* A giant geyser exploded upward, and hot, glowing lava shot into the sky.

All across *Sugar Rush,* the cy-bugs flew toward the burning light and vaporized. Even Turbo could not escape. His cy-bug body dragged him into the lava, and *ZAP!* He was cy-bug toast, just like the others.

We had won!

I still had one more thing to take care of: Vanellope needed to cross the finish line. Felix had fixed her kart as good as new.

When Vanellope rolled across the line, the game reset itself. All the destruction caused by the cy-bugs was repaired. Everything and everyone was brand-new and sparkling! And Vanellope stood before the residents of *Sugar Rush* in a beautiful princess gown, complete with a crown and wand.

"All hail the Rightful Ruler of *Sugar Rush:* Princess Vanellope!" Sour Bill proclaimed.

All the racers rushed up.

"Hey, Vanellope, you know all that

stuff we said earlier was a joke, right?" said Taffyta.

Vanellope grinned wickedly. "I hereby decree that anyone who was ever mean to me shall be . . . immediately executed!"

The racers burst into tears.

"I'm just kidding!" Vanellope said. She pulled off her crown and glitched back to her old self, the cheeky little kid I loved.

Vanellope didn't want to be a princess and give up her glitching. Glitching was her superpower!

The arcade was about to open. It was time for all of us to get back to our games.

"You could just stay here and live in the castle," Vanellope said wistfully. "You could be happy."

But I was already happy. I had the coolest friend in the world. And besides, I had a job. It might not be a fancy job, like being princess. But it was mine!

Felix and I made it back to the *Fix-It Felix Jr.* game just seconds before Mr. Litwak was about to unplug it. As he and a little kid watched the screen, I popped up.

"I'M GONNA WRECK IT!" I said.

"Fix it, Felix!" the Nicelanders cried.

Our game was saved, and I was back where I belonged. But some things changed.

Felix and Sergeant Calhoun got married. And we invited some of the homeless characters from Game Central to be extras in our game as a bonus level. I built homes for them using the bricks from my brick pile.

I'm still the Bad Guy. I still wreck buildings and get dumped into mud puddles. But now everyone likes me. I even get a cake with a little figurine of me on the roof wearing a medal. I am everyone's favorite Bad Guy.

Best of all, each time I get thrown off the roof, I get a perfect view of *Sugar Rush*. I

can see Vanellope racing. She's a natural. All the other players love her, just like I knew they would.

I know now that I don't need a medal to prove I'm a good guy. Because if that little kid likes me, how bad can I be?